ZER

Two rooms for two, please.
　Sure, give me a sec.
　Shoot, I don't have it, I left my wallet at home. Boul?
Matt?
　Can you please pay for both of us?
　Hey, don't start, alright?
　You got it, Boul.
　Ding-ding-ding!!
　Sir, give me a sec, please.
　Again, a sec?
　Two secs.
　You mean sovs.
　No, secs.
　Sex? You into kinky stuff, mate?
　No, I just asked you to
　What the hell is he talking about, Matt?
　Fuck knows, I only have my debit card.
　Amex?
　Amen.
　Oh, my Dog...
　Lobby boy? Lobby boy?
　Matt, leave him alone.
　Is he turning or what?
　We ain't busy, are we?
　I know, Boul but, *ding ding ding!!*
　Sir, I'm right in front of you, I can perfectly hear what you're saying.
　Can you now?

I could even before.
Ah.
Aha!
GIVE US THE BLOODY ROOOOOM!!!
Boul, don't shout, for Christ's sake!
I know, I'm so sorry, I don't usually...
Hey, he's turning, he's

Matt?
Lloyd?
Matt? What are you doing here?
No, Lloyd, what is You doing here?
This is my Hotel.
You don't say.
I do.
The Lloyd Hotel.
Precisely.
Fack me.
What are you doing here?
Well, I came with
Sir, London Boulevardier!
Yes, I was just about to...
Hello to you, my loyal friend, Lloyd.
Is that really you?
Flesh and blood.
Unbelievable!
I know, it's been a while but now I'm back.
December 30th. Wow. What are you two darlings doing here!?
What are we doing here?
Yeah, what...
Lloyd,
are...
if you ask it again,

you...
I swear I'll
doing here?
Kill you!
None of your business, Lloyd.
Yeah, none of your facking biz, o'aigh?
Matt, can you please drop the loser mobster attitude for once?
You go' i' boss.
It's such a pleasure to see you again, sir.
Lloyd, Lloyd, Lloyd.
London Boulevardier, London Boulevardier, London Boulevardier.
Lloyd.
Yes?
Don't call me sir, call me Mr London Boulevardier.
Easier, innit?
Matt, let him speak.
No.
No what, Lloyd?
I mean, yes, of course.
Yes of course what, Lloyd??
Shut up, Matt.
Indeed, I will call you Mr London Boulevardier, sir.
Oh my...
Lloyd, are we supposed to spend the night in front of this goddamn counter?
Matt?
It's me.
Aww, sure! Do you want a room?
Finally...

Sir?
Ask me, ask me, ask me, Lloyd.
About the room, do you want...

Ask me, I won't say no, how could I?
Two?
No.
A single and a double?
No.
Two singles?
No.
Two doubles then?
Lloyd, we don't want nofing, innit?
Shut up, Matt.
Do you want a triple plus a single special, sir?
Do you have them, Lloyd?
No, I'm sorry, Mr London Boulevardier, the hotel is fully booked.
Fackin hell, Lloyd, so why did you even bother to...
Er...
That's okay, we're just waiting anyway.
For what/who/when, sir, if I may?
You may not, Lloyd.
But...
Tut-tut.
Lloyd?
Matt?
Mr Boulevardier?
Lloyd?
Please take a seat in the lobby as we prepare the room for you.
What room, for fuck's sake?

| 02

"I feel like, I don't know... like I could rule the world and no longer be at the mercy of Narcolepsy for I have found in Sue the Somnambulist, my new girlfriend, the perfect companion on my nocturnal travels;

For when I am walking in the woods, often with other creatures of the night, or when I am slip-sliding through the wet side streets and alleys of the East End and hoping to avoid a conversation with Jack, who like many of his peers in the aristocracy is rather boring, always talking about the perfect knife for his hobby.

I cannot remain awake for his neurodiverse explanations and, unfortunately, I fall asleep at his feet.

It is Sue, good old sleep-walking Sue, who finds me, usually tucked into a coal bin, and carries me home.

Now if only she could remember where I live."

ON | E

Okay... what the hell was that?
What, Matt?
Didn't you hear it, Lloyd?
No.
Boulevardier?
Matt, what are you talking about?
The voices. The coal bin. The narco something guy who...
Wait, are you sure it was a guy?
Brilliant question, Boul. Brilliant question.
I know. Go on, Matt.
Where was I?
Voices. Sleepless girl.
Yes, this woman getting lost around alleys and, hey!!
Hey what?
Boul, didn't you say you heard nothing?
I didn't.
You didn't hear shit or you didn't say you...
I didn't.
You didn't do what when, Boul, when??
May I interrupt?
NOOOO!!
Good, since you two shouted at me at once, the shout doesn't count.
In which world is that a rule, Lloyd?
Isn't it obvious, Matt?
It's not, Lloyd.
Marvellous, thanks for supporting me, sir.

I didn't.

As I was saying, the voices you heard were most probably coming from room 56.

So, you heard that fucking psycho!

Man or woman, Matt?

Bould, that's not the point.

I know. This is the point.

Uh?

.

Ah.

Are you done, you two?

What's up, Lloyd?

Don't you understand that this Hotel, my hotel is haunt...

Boul?

Matt?

Did Lloyd just freeze?

Shtum. I agree, Matt.

Lloyd?

What were you saying? Lloyd?

Er... nothing. Nothing, really.

Well, it was something. Something, really.

Please take a seat in the lobby. I will be there to serve you in a sec.

Triple sec.

Quadruple sec for me!!

Indeed, Matt and indeed, sir. I'll do what I can.

Great.

Grunt.

If you would like to follow me...

TW | O

Gentlemen, I might be able to give you one of the themed rooms. Asap, I hope, anyway.
  Wow, thanks Lloyd.
  Which one?
  Well, Matt, I was thinking the California room would do great for you so,
  Sunshiyain...
  Where?
  Surfboards and hot chicks...
  Is he high?
  Nah, Lloyd, he simply spaced out.
  Ah. Where?
  Baywatch. The American drama television series about lifeguards who patrol the beaches of Los Angeles County, California, and Hawaii, starring David Hasselhoff.
  I get it, sir. Girls, Summer, boobs.
  Watch your language.
  Yes, sir, sorry, sir.
  As you were, Lloyd.
  I simply meant it featured Pamela Anderson.
  And David Hasselhoff.
  Clearly. Now, if you guys want to check in, I'll have a member of staff to take you there.
  Where?
  To your California dreaming room.

As Lloyd said those words, a very precise memory from the past emerged from nowhere far and indelibly entered the eyes of everyone.

Matt
Mr B
Matt
Mr B
Matt
Mr B. Shall we stop whispering?
Okay, Matt. Tell it like it is.
There she stood in the doorway.
I thought I heard her tell Lloyd that we're from heaven or we're from hell.
Are you sure you want to stay, Mr B?
Hell yes, Matt, she reminds me of someone...
Yeah! And me, but for the life of me I can't remember.
Matt, she lit up a candle, she's showing us the way!
Mr B, did you hear her voice along the corridor?
Yes Matt I thought I heard her say,
Welcome to the Hotel Lloyd
Such a lovely face
And you, Mr Youth, have a lovely face
Have you forgotten me
Welcome to the Hotel Lloyd
Any time of year
You can find me here
Aaand why not Hotel Lloyd.
Why not indeed, Mr B, it's the Scandi version of New York's Chelsea Hotel
Matt! I remember.
Mr B! I forget.
Some dance to remember,
Some dance to forget.

I remember it was a different time:
Pigalle in Paris 1969.
I was there, Mr B, I was in love with a waitress!
I too, was in love with a beautiful waitress.
I feel a Bowie moment has arrived.
Oh no, don't say it's true.
Yes, indeed we were in love with the same waitress and that's her!
Yeah... let's go talk to her.

ARTZON | E

I remember
December 11:58 pm 1978
Paris St. Germain
I said...
She said...
I said...
She said 'Remember the innocence of strawberries ...'

THRE | E

Talk to her?
 Yes.
 Talk to her??
 Yes.
 Talk to her???
 Yes, Matt.
 Fuck no.
 Fuck yes, Matt!
 Why?
 Because I told you, she reminds me of…
 Blab blab blab, o'aigh, o'aigh, we're going!
 Where?
 I don't know, you said…
 AH!
 AHA!
 I remember, the waiter!
 She's gone, Boul.
 No way.
 Yes way.
 Waaaaaaaaaaaaaaaait!! Her!
 Guys?
 Lloyd?
 Can you keep it low?
 Profile?
 Volume.
 Lloyd, Lloyd Lloyd.
 Matt?

Aren't we paying?
Actually...
So we can fuck-king do what-eva we fuck-king want. Innit?
Actually...
Matt, where's the waiter? Can you see her?
Kinda busy at the mo, Mr Boulevardier, innit?
Can you see her?
No.
Liar.
Lloyd, are we square?
Matt, for the last time, the Hotel is fully booked, you didn't pay and there is no waiter whatsoever in here, never been, never will. Especially not since the acc...
What did you just say, my loyal friend Lloyd?
Sir?
You mentioned an acc...
Boul, let's not lose focus on what's important here.
My beloved waiter?
No. Our one-two-three-you tell me, bedroom suite.
What suite? Who's paying, Matt?
Tut-tut. You, of course.
Never!
Lloyd? No suite?
I told you straight away, Matt. Fully booked.
Oh, shut up, there must be 187 rooms here.
201, to be precise.
And not a spare bed for your pals?
As I said, I might have...
When?
If you would follow me to the lobby, I...
Lloyd!
Sir?

You say fully booked, I say I can hear no sounds whatsoever. No one's wandering around. We haven't stumbled into/bumped into/encountered a soul since we arrived. And you say...
Fully booked.
How come?
Good question, sir.
Thanks.
Would you please follow me to the lobby?
I don't know... Mr Boulevardier?
Yes?
This way, please.
I think we shall follow our friend, Matt.
Okay, boss, though...
What now?
I think I...
What now??
Wait, wait.
What???
Didn't we forget something?
Indeed, Matt, indeed.
I agree.
Not now, Lloyd.
We most definitely may have had, Matt!
So what is it, Boul?
You tell me.
Something like...
You tell me.
A...
You tell me.
The title?
You tell
Okay, I fucking tell you, yes, yes, I facking get it, Boul!!!!
Wasn't he accepted into the program?

The anger management programme you mean, Lloyd?
That's the one!
SHUTTA FUKKA!!!
Yes, Matt?
Guys, don't you get it?
No.
We're missing the bloody core of this book!!
So let's launch it!
What? Whaaaaat Boul????
The credits, isn't it clear, Matt?
Uh?
:

PRODUCTIONS
PRESENTS:

A ~~FILM~~ BOOK BY

Matt Charlton
Youth Francis

LAST NIGHT AT THE
LLOYD HOTEL

MATT YOUTH - FRANCIS CHARLTON

Copyright © Matt Youth & Francis Charlton 2025

All rights reserved.

Matt Youth has asserted his right to be identified as the author
of this Work in accordance with the Copyright
Designs and Patents Act 1988

Francis Charlton has asserted his right to be identified as the author
of this Work in accordance with the Copyright
Designs and Patents Act 1988

ISBN: 9798312897913

This book is a work of fiction. In some cases true life
figures appear but their actions and conversations are entirely fictitious.
All other characters, and all names of places and descriptions of events,
are the product of the author's imagination and any resemblance to
actual persons or places are entirely coincidental.

For Eloise
My Inspiration

- - - - - - -

For Midable!
Oh, yeah.

'The distant echo
of faraway voices boarding faraway trains'
Paul Weller

Last Night At The
LLOYD HOTEL

Matt Charlton is a mythological creature that was never born in 2022 and will never die, floating forever among the Olympus of the undead, the rockstars, Jesus, God, Buddha and, you know, the lot.
Innit? is Matt Charlton's masterpiece so far but this isn't it, innit? This is better. Better than nothing. This is the Definitive Masterpiece. Until the next one. So,
STAY WIRED
Anyway, don't trust me, nor the authorities nor, especially, mum.
Do listen to the YouTubers, the Influencers and other real people who talk about real stuff on TikTok. Since we're famous as f****uck, we got tons of rave-views for our novella. Here is the top of the pops selection of those

RAVE | VIEWS

Sorry, no rave-views available at the moment.

Please Refresh

Refresh

Refresh

Refresh

Refresh

Refresh

Refresh

Refresh

Refresh

Refresh

Refresh

Refresh

Refresh

Refresh

Refresh

Refresh

Refresh

Refresh

Refresh

Refresh

Refresh

Refresh

Refresh

Refresh

Refresh

Right, whatever.
Let's meet the authors.

ROGUE
MILE END

FRANCIS CHARLTON **IS AN ARTIST, POET AND SO-CALLED** WRITER. HE IS **CURRENTLY IN PROTECTIVE CUSTODY WHILE THE OLD BILL INVESTIGATE ALLEGATIONS** THAT HE IS **PURSUING A VENDETTA** AGAINST, WHAT ARE LAUGHINGLY CALLED, MIME ARTISTES.

"Art" by Matt Youth
Graphic bollocks by Matt Charlton
Want a free poster? Rip this page and paste it onto your walls
Aight? You're welcome.

ROGUE
MILE END

MATT YOUTH
A K A
MATT YOUTH
IS A WANNABE
WRITER
ROCKNROLLER
AND OTHER
THINGS YOU
**DON'T
WANNA
KNOW**
AH, AND HE PROUDLY
NEVER SOLD
ANY OF HIS SO-CALLED
BOOKS
SO PLEASE
DON'T EVER BUY
THIS ONE TOO

Art by Francis Charlton
Graphic bollocks by Matt Charlton
Want a free poster? Rip this page and paste it onto your walls
Aight? You're welcome

FOU | R

So, where were we?

ARTZ | ONE

The Art Zone...

Picture of two artists, and more importantly good friends, looking at a picture of a beautiful woman of another time, a once brilliant star in a firmament no longer a part of the sky, eclipsed by the movement of earth and time.

Ella Jennystan, who both of the artists loved, whose world is a studio, whose dreams are made out of sketches, and drawings. Ella Jennystan: struck down by hit-and-run years and lying on the pavement, trying desperately to get the registration number of Shoreditch Twat, the so-called Modern Artist.

Where is she now? They both exclaim. What happened to her?

To Ella Jennystan, class of 69 Pop Artist / Waitress, she's always been here living, painting waitressing in a studio next to Hotel Lloyd. It can only happen in the Art Zone.

F | IVE

I'm not exactly me at the moment, I'm a little Boulevardier, a lot Matt Youth. There's probably, maybe 9% of the real me remaining, I'm a shadow of my former self, I've become obsessed with so-called Modern Art and as the real me fades and I wave bye-bye, I realise I'm channelling David Bowie lyrics again! Fuck me. I thought I was cured.

Odd that it all began at the regular Mill Town Arts Salon in the Hebden Bridge Town Hall Café, or did it?

Matt Youth remembers turning up at the Blue Teapot in Mytholmroyd where we were discussing modern art, déjà vu indeed.

Matt Youth remembers turning up at the Blue Teapot in Mytholmroyd where we were discussing modern art, déjà vu indeed.

'You'll laugh, you'll cry,' I say, 'you may even buy one of Matt's prints or a copy of our book to remind you of the day' I ran screaming into the Thursday market crowds warning people that there were lunatic artists loose in Hebden Bridge.

And suddenly you realise that they are talking about you.

I'm not exactly me at the moment, apparently I was shouting, 'Listen to me! Please listen! If you don't, if you won't, if you fail to understand, then the same incredible terror that's menacing me will strike at you.'

'What was this Terror?' You rightly ask? 'Well, let me put it into perspective for you: it's modern art. Yes, modern art. If the so-called creative calls what he does art then it's art. I ask you. What the fuck? Just saying.'

My only hope was to get away from Hebden Bridge to get to the M62 to warn the others of what was happening.

'Help! Wait! Stop! Stop and listen to me!'

These people who're coming after me are not truly artists! Look, you fools, you're in danger! Can't you see?! They're after you! They're after all of us! Our wives, our children, There is nothing to hold onto, except each other. They come from another world, Shoreditch, actually, and they are insatiable, spending all of their money on crap and calling it modern art.

I couldn't just sit there while they are measuring me for a straightjacket, I've got to do something! Call for help! Oh, what's the use? Doctor, will you tell these fools? I'm not crazy. Make them listen to me before it's too late. But things don't really change, I'm standing in the wind, but I never wave bye-bye. But I try. I try, and the last thing I remember was me screaming...

S | IX

Ahhhhhhhhhhhhhhhh!
What? What, Matt?
Where? Where, Matt?
The pill. In the now.
That makes sense.
Yes, Boul, I finally remember.
Matt, would you please stop calling me that?
The pill did it, Boul. That, and your monologue.
What the hell are you talking about?
You don't know?
I can't know what I don't know, right, Matt?
You snoozed out for a while, Mr Boulevardier.
Do what, Lloyd?
You tuned out, Boul. But you made me remember I couldn't forget.
To take the pill?
Yes. And that other thing.
Lloyd, did you poison Matt with some of your alcoholic concoctions?
A Martini, you mean?
I meant beer.
No sir, that would kill him. He gets high on decaf cappuccinos, sir
Indeed. Indeed, Lloyd. A London Pride for me then.
Sure, if only you would follow me to the lobby I...
I almost forgot to remember, guys. Remember?
No, Matt. Not really.
Forget to Remember, that's the song we wrote when we started.

We?
Mr Boulevardier, sir, you were in a band?
Gang?
It was my band, my teenage youth. Sonic. Those years I now embrace and recall. And the ghost, yes, the gh... no way!
What? Where? When?
There!!
A spirit?
Bang Bang Bang, you're dead!
Who for goodness sake, Matt?
The ghost!
What ghost for goodness sake, Matt?
The ghost, the ghost! And argh... sorry, I missed.
ATTENTION PLEASE!
Lloyd?
Ladies and gents,
Yes?
I swear to God there are no such things as ghosts, spectres, phantoms,
Wraiths?
No!
Odd presences?
Nooo, not in my hotel, the Lloyd Hotel.
Of course there aren't, why would you say that?
I...
Why would you...
There, *Bang*, fucking *Bang*, mega xl-fucking *Bang!*
Ahhhhhhhh
Uhhhhhhh
Yiiiiiiiii
Did you get it?
I did! Almost...
The ghost? Dead?

What ghost? Is this place haunted?
NO IT'S NOT!!! IT'S NAAAAAAAT!!!
Matt, you said, wait... Lloyd?
Sir?
Are you insane? For the life of me, I never heard you shouting like that.
I did?
You did.
You totally did, Lloyd, shame on you. Disgrace on you. Cataclysm on you.
...
Whatever. Guys, we need to celebrate the more or less killing of my future-old-me ghost!
Your future old what?
Motherfucker's been chasing me till I said bye-bye to kindergarten.
Oh, you mean that ghost.
Yes, Boulevardier, precisely that lurid mother frother.
Then, we need to celebrate, Matt.
Yes, Boul, we need indeed.
What's so bad about that specific ghost?
Specific you say, Lloyd?
Er...
Everything's bad about it. Where the fuck have you been all of your life, Lloyd?
Inside... my... hotel?
You never met the future-old-you ghost?
Er... no?
Sit down:
I am already.
Great. It's the dreamless, futureless, motivationless you. The one stealing your hopes, the bully punching you in the face as he grabs all the sweets off your still immaculate kid's hands;
Ah.

It's the shadow trying to black and white your rainbowy future when you're small, the same one hovering over your teenage days and it's him again when you get old, in case you still haven't surrendered. That's the voice that constantly whispers "you're not a kid anymore"
Fuck him!
"You can't play no more"
Fuck the fucker!
"Grow up!"
Noooooooo never!!!!!!
... loudly, inside your innocent ears, subtly dragging your creativity down into a viscous gasoline pond, bottomless, capable of staining your child-pure soul for good;
Monster.
He can't stand inventiveness. Can't allow imagination.
Kill the bastard!
Hallelujah, let's kill the bastard!
Youth! Matt Youth!
What's my name again?
Youth! Matt Youth!
I can't hear you!
YOUTH! MATT YOUTH!!
One more time!!
YOUUUTH!!!!!
YOUUUUUUUTH!!!!!
YAAAAAAAAAAAAAAAAATH!!!!!
Let's praise the Lord, folks!
(and someone calls an ambulance for Lloyd)
Gents, the situation requires a toast.
Yeah, sir, booze, booze, to the lobbyyyyyyy!
Is he okay?
Not the least, Boul.
Right. Shall we drink to immortality, Matt?

To youth. The youth of the spirit.
"We live till we die. We die when we stop living."
Bravo, Mr London Boulevardier!
Thanks, Lloyd.
Now, shall we move into the lobby?
Do you still have it with you, Boul?
What Matt, the ghost?
Hell yeah.
Always. Clung to my shoulder like the worst of diseases. A god damn vulture if you ask me. Every day I flap my wings and he grasps my ankle. Sometimes I win, sometimes I lose.
A nightmare.
Sometimes you live, sometimes you're dead.
Couldn't have said it better, Boul, let's drink our lives away!
Shall we move into the lobby then?
Lloyd, if you say lobby once again I swear I'll make clear to anyone what's inside a bloody Mary.
Point non-taken, sir, but... okay.
Brilliant. Now, bring 6 London Pride and 6 more as chasers.
For the three of us?
No, for me. Who's paying, by the way?
It's on the house, sir.
Aww, so make it 18 Pride and 18 chasers then.
For the three of us?
No, Lloyd, for me. Are you even listening?
My apologies.
And shake an Appletini for yourself too, my friend.
I'm sorry, sir, I can't drink on the job.
Bullshit. I can't not drink on the job!
Painting you mean?
You should try sometime, Lloyd.
Painting you mean?
Yes, yes, yes! You're getting annoying, Lloyd. Let's drink.
Indeed, sir.

Matt, what are you having for your victory toast?
Please pour me a glassful of bubbles, fuck it I'm gonna get high tonight.
Champagne?
Sparkling water, Lloyd.
Decaffeinated sparkling water?
Do you have some?
No, well... no. I was only joking.
So, now you're into discriminating people ainch'a, you bloody immigrant, coloured, gay, woman, innit?
I'm a straight white male from Leicester, Matt.
Shame on you, Lloyd. Shame on you.
I know, I apologise.
You better.
Yes, Matt. Guys, are we all set?
Never.
Marvellous, Mr Boulevardier. Please, take a seat. I'll be with you in a sec.

ARTZO | NE

Hi, Matt, are you coming out tonight?
Nah, I haven't got any clean clothes.
Is your girlfriend still in Roma?
Yep, visiting her parents for another month.
It's not funny, you know.
I know. It's serious.
There were times when she could have washed and ironed our clothes and times when I could have murdered a cup of tea but she was too busy packing to make me a cup.
Did you have an argument?
Yes, I walked out, I was manic on the streets of London, she called an Uber, phoned from the airport when she arrived, she was upset, incoherent, obviously manic on the streets of Roma.
And I wonder to myself, could we ever be the same again?
But she's manic on the streets of Roma, Milano, Firenze and I wonder to myself:
Should I turn off the voiceover and hang the painting of her by that Boulevardier chap, because it says nothing to me about my wife.
Because it's not realistic, then it's the portrait, the portrait, the portrait, the portrait...
That will bring us together.

SEV | EN

Lloyd, give me 5 minutes and we'll continue...
 Are you alright, Mr B?
 Fine, Matt, a little tired perhaps, Ivanka can be very demanding, and this sofa is so soft that I'm going to take a 4 minute power nap.
 Okay, Mr B, I'll stay with you and help myself to your beer.
 Indeed you will, Matt, prego, my friend.
 Grazie. Mr B?

(Voice over) *Witness, if you will, as one of the protagonists takes a well-deserved snooze, little realising he'd fallen asleep in the Art Zone*

Arhhhhhhhhhhhhhhhhhhhh!
 Screams the Boulevardier waking from a nightmare.
 Mr B, you alright? Can I be of assistance?
 The Boulevardier looks around and rubs his eyes:
 Matt, it's you, I was just dreaming about you, and your Found Musicians student project. Remember the time you channelled Morrissey...
 The Boulevardier stalls, he could feel a *tap, tap*, tapping of someone lightly touching his shoulder and, turning to confront whoever was now poking him,:
 Who are you? I've not seen you before and why do you look like an 80-year-old Lloyd?
 I am the Concierge for Hotel Lloyd and I've always been here, as you yourselves have always been here...

EIGH | T

I'm not.
You're not what, Matt?
I haven't been here since the birth of time. I'm not old like you two chaps.
Lads, you mean.
Call yourselves whatever. I don't belong here.
Calm down, please.
Sir, Matt probably just had a simple, innocent vision of some spir...
Say it again, Lloyd?
It's the beer. I said he's under the spell of...
Spell, Lloyd?
Er... the spirit, I mean, alcohol... didn't he have a sip of your Asahi, Mr Boulevardier?
Oh, he did indeed! Look at that!
At what?
The level! It was here when I snoozed out!
Right below the label?
Yes, yes, Lloyd!! See?
It's still there, sir.
Noooo, no no no, he drank it, you don't know Matt, but I do. He did it, the rogue!
Indeed, sir.
Shut up you two, I barely wet my lips with that thing.
Beer. It's beer, Matt!
I know. I. Know. And I'm also pretty sure-ish I either saw you two wearing Halloween masks of 80 y.o. yous or it was the exact

same thing but... real. In any case, let's face it, this place is haunted.
AH. BOLLOCKS!
Lloyd?
You said us two, correct?
Yes, you two, I know what I saw, Lloyd.
Hahaha U2. Are you going to a concert, Matt?
Well...
Nobody's going anywhere! Not until someone explains to me, the London Boulevardier, what the hell's wrong with this place.

It's you.
hissed a fully reverb-ed deep voice.
Shivers.

What did you say, Lloyd?
Me, sir?
Yeah you, goddammit!
I was shtum, Matt.
You were?
I was.
You weren't.
I was.
I don't believe a word you said, Lloyd!
No, I, don't believe a word you said!
Oh, you sneaky...
Lloyd, enough with the chit-chat, where is my Pride?
Pride?
Lost a thousand years ago, innit, Boul?
Are you talking to me, Matt?
I am.
Are you talking to me, Matt?
Pretty sure I am.

Are you talking to me, M...
Quick! Unplug him, Lloyd!
Uh?
He got stuck.
Like a broken record?
Yeah he does that.
Are you talking to
Zzzzp
Peach dark.
Yummyiiiii dessert!!!!
No, Matt, I mean... where are you?
I can't see shit! Boul?
Matt?
Lloyd? What the fuck did you unplug?
Unplug? What's going on?
You pulled something and the London Boulevardier... you got him in a permanent frozen state!
Do what?
Plus the lights, you switched off the whole fucking Hotel!
Lloyd!!!
Can't see shit.
I know, Boul, we're working on it.
Can't see shit, Matt.
I got your message, man.
Can't see sh...
LLOYD LLOOOOOOOYD LOOOYYYYD FOR CHRIST's SAKE, LOOK WHAT YOU'VE DONE!!! HE'S TALKING LIKE ME, REPLUG THIS BLOODY SHACK, NOW!!!!

Can't.
Said the odd, grave voice again; fear dripped from the damask wallpapered walls; panic injected the eyes of the many Lords trapped in their framed oil portraits on canvas; darkness soaked

the already clouded skies which hovered among the meanders of Matt's and the Boulevardier's craniums, like a veil of mist.

And the universe got silent for a snap long the length of a thousand snaps. The whole building was jet black, no living soul appeared to be breathing around that so-called fully booked, crammed Hotel with hundreds of rooms.

Lloyd?

Asked Matt and the London Boulevardier at once, holding their hands under the cover of darkness.

Lloyd?

But Lloyd was nowhere in sight.

N | INE

It was dea...
Shhhh!
Boul?
Don't say it.
Death?
NOOOOOOOOO.
I...
NOOOOOOOOO.
But...
NOOOOOOOOO.
And...
NOOOOOOOOO.
Okay, I said it, so what?
So wh... look, if you want to jinx it, jinx it for yourself, leave me out of it, alright?
Oh, come on, Boul, don't tell me you're superstitious now.
... and then. And before. Not just now. I've always been me if that's what you're asking.
It wasn't.
Great.
Marvellous.
...
So, if it wasn't the end, what the hell is going on here?
It must be one of those blackouts.
Sure. One that blackouts only this room, innit?
What are you saying, Matt?
I bet there's still light and music and dancers upstairs.
Still? Dancers?

I know, we haven't seen a single soul around. Yet...
Right, I see where you're going with this, Matt.
Downstairs?
No, I mean
Upstairs?
No can do.
Not even if I say that there's a li'l bathroom window we could use to exit this place and end up somewhere else, like, I don't know, one floor above upstairs?
Is such a window for real?
Definitely maybe!
Right, I appreciate your precarious certainty forward slash enthusiasm, Matt, but even if what you say is true we still can't, can we?
I know, but...
No butts. We have to sit in here till she/he/it arrives.
Or they, you forgot they!
Okay, okay, until they arrive.
How many?
What?
How many are they?
One, it's one god damn entity, Matt!
So why did you say it plural?
You bast... you tricked me into this!
Boul, calm down, we have to be fluid, genderless, modern these days, don't you get it?
Argh...
You should TikTok more, insta pixa on X, xxx.
I swear, I...
Don't get angry, Boul. Chillax, man.
AAAARGH!!! You and your unlaughable jokes, I'M SICK OF

bzzzzzzztzttzttzzzz

Lloyd? Is that you?
...
Did you unplug him for real this time?
...
Lloyd?
..
Lloyd??
.
Lloyd???

AR | TZONE

Consider this, if you will, for Ella Jennystan artist and muse to Dave Boulevard, going to bed in London and waking up in Casablanca, could only happen in the Art Zone

The Uber drops her at Dave's Studio and Bar.
    Of all the Art Studios, in all the towns, in all the world, she walks into mine...
    What do you mean by that, Dave?
    Ella, she's just walked in.
    Dave, what are you going to say?
    The truth, Matt, the truth, Ella. It doesn't take much to see that the problems of three artists don't amount to a hill of beans in this crazy world. Someday you'll understand that.
    Will I, Dave?
    Wanksta© is watching the CCTV. He sees Ella arguing with Dave.
    Now, now, says Dave and gently places his hand under her chin and raises it so their eyes meet.
    Here's looking at you, Ella, I've finished the portrait.
    Just paint it once, Dave. For Matt's sake.
    I don't know what you mean, Ella.
    Paint it, Dave. Paint it. Paint it because as time goes by, Matt will forget me and you said you would paint me again.
    I can't remember how many I've painted, Ella.
    Paint me naked again. You must remember this, a canvas is just a canvas, a paint brush is just a brush. The fundamental things apply, as time goes by, Matt will forget. He won't remember who,

he'll forget you, I love you. I'll paint you on that you can rely, no matter what that implies.
Dave, I thought I told you never to paint Ella again.
Okay, but...
No but's, Dave.
Ella. Kiss me. Kiss me as if it were the last time, as I'm off through the bathroom window.
There's something you should know before you leave.
I don't ask you to explain anything.
Dave, I'm going to anyway because it may make a difference to you later on. You said you knew about Ella and me.
Yes.
What you didn't know was that she was at my place last night when you were painting. She came there for some zinc white, isn't that true, Ella?
Yes.
She tried everything to get a tube. She did her best to convince me she was still in love with me but that was over long ago. For your sake, she pretended it wasn't and I let her pretend.
I understand.
Here it is, Dave.
Thanks. I appreciate it.
Are you ready, Ella?
Yes, I'm ready. Good-bye, Matt, Godard bless you.
You better hurry. You'll miss that Uber.

TE | N

Loud snoring is heard off stage, camera pans down, the mic picks up the Boulevardier talking in his sleep

I must be dreaming or am I awake or dreaming I'm dreaming I'm awake. I still love her, she's mine, I must talk with Matt. Matt, where are you?
  I'm here right next to you.
  Hugh. You who.
  You hoo! Hi.
  You're not, Matt, LLOYD! Lloyd, what are you doing there?
  I was sleeping until you began talking to yourself and Ella.
  Stop me, stop me if you think that I've said this before. Nothing's changed, Lloyd, I still love Ella.
  What are you saying, Mr. Boulevardier?
  Oh, I still love you and Matt, only slightly less than I used to.
  What happened?
  The Uber was late, I was delayed, I was way-laid.
  I started to drink too much, I slept outside the brewery waiting for them to open the gates, the guard said you used to be so proud.
  I shouted at him, don't you understand I've no Pride, point me to the trolleys.
  And then what did you do?
  Well, Lloyd, for 60 minutes I was happy in the haze of a drunken hour but heaven knows I'm happy now. I was looking for Ella and then I found her and heaven knows I'm happy now.

In my studio, I give valuable time to portraits of Ella and I don't want to live a lie.
Good for you.
Don't patronise me, Lloyd for heaven knows I'm happy now. I was looking for Matt and then I found Ella and heaven knows Matt's miserable now.
And if a Turner Prize is in the works to paint by your side is such a heavenly way to win the prize.
And if a pallet of ten litres of sky blue is enough for the both of us then to paint by your side, well, the pleasure, the privilege is mine.
It certainly is, Mr Boulevardier.
Well, thank you, Lloyd.
You're welcome.
So, you're Hugh Lloyd the mythical owner of Art Hotels worldwide?
I may be, or I'm a figment of your imagination, like MYouth.
Who's he.
He is your best friend.
No, Matt is my best friend.
You are Matt.
No, I am the Boul...

Alarms sound
Camera slowly pulls back
Calm electronic voice says

CODE SIX CODE SIX
CODE SIX CODE SIR
CODE SIX CODE SIX
CODE SIX

Sound fades
Sudden loud sound of a continuous

Monotone
Beeep

Screen goes black

EL | EVEN

So, you the owner of Art Hotels, innit?
Matt!
Yeah, I know who I am.
Who are you talking to?
Lloyd?
I'm the Boulevardier, Matt.
Sorry, with this darkness I can see shit.
You can't.
That's what I said.
No, it's not. I might be affected by sudden, violent and catastrophic snoring attacks but I most certainly am not deaf.
Yet.
What?
What time is it, Boul?
How can I possibly know it, Matt?
What do you mean?
Don't you see the world's completely blacked out?
No, I don't see shit.
Aha!
Look, Boul.
Where?
I'm getting sick of this situation, don't we have something like a bunch of matches or
A flamethrower?
Do you have one?
Nah, confiscated last year.
Bollocks.
True story, Matt!

No, Boul, what I meant is:
Yes?
Where the fucking fuck is LOOOOOYD?
WHAT??
I'M NOT TALKING TO YOU, BOUL!!!
AH!
THANK GOODNESS YOU WEREN'T DEAF!!
I'M NOT, MATT!
OKKAAAY!!
LLOYD, bring your fat Lou Reed ass back in here you bloody bas...

Frsssssh!

Hissed something behind a wall.
　? asked Matt
　?? asked the London Boulevardier

Crrrssssss

Replied the same wall, only a few inches further down, on the left.

Frsssssh!!!!

Bellowed the entity possessing that creaking decadent wallpapered wall and: kaboom!

VAMP!!

the one candle, perfectly melted over the third shelf of the dusty lobby library, started dripping light again, upside down,

smudging the faces, smoothing the corners and dirtying the carpet with its trembling, shaky dancing shadows.
Fuuuuuuuck.
Matt?
Fuuuuuuuuuck.
What was that?
Fuuuuuuuuuuuuuuuck.
You said that already.
Unbelievable.
I know.
I know.
We know.
Holy shit, is it...
No it's not, how many times do I have to repeat it to you?
What time is it, Boul?
It's precisely fuck do I know o'clock, okay?
Please, don't swear.
Don't? Don't?? You made me!
Boul, what time is it?
Why??
You know why!
Matt, she's never on time, she isn't that kind but one thing is for sure:
Say it!
she always has to interrupt the fun.
That's her style, innit?
Death doesn't come early, especially not when you're in a rush.
Like Santa?
Like Santa.
Still, what time is it, Boul?

It's 20 seconds to 20 seconds ago

Croaked a mysterious raspy voice, oozing from the very one wall behind them two lonely, only guests of the Lloyd Hotel.
Panic.
Matt jumped on his feet.
The London Boulevardier didn't give a fuck.

He took a sipful of his Asahi and ranted: "speak, speak if you dare", without turning, not slightly, to the talking surface living on his back.

#1 | 6

Hotel room
　Floor's blue
　Like the ocean
　With fishes
　Only it's plastic
　And it sucks
　And it don't swim
　And it don't fish
　Fishes
　Swishing forward
　No more
　Nor ever
　It's
　What??
　My Propeller
　In a fucking travellodge
　I'm the whore of myself
　I'll date the shit out of me
　If only I could
　Invite me over
　There!
　What?
　Fuck!!
　Ahhhhhh
　Ohhhhhh
　Ihhhhhh
　Uhhhhh
　Ehhhh

Yikes!
Yuck
Burp.
And that was it
The summarisation of
A night on
The highway
Mattress of white
Noise
Buzzy cloud
Cushioning the night and
The day
You o'aight, mate?
Asks one guest to another
In the lobby
Rum
And coke
And glasses
And the unstoppable flow of
The highway
No way
Stream of unconsciousness
Constantly streamed by
Thousands of drivers who
Drive their shit around
Making a hypnotic sound
That sounds like
And what the fuck was that??
Where??
There!
Shit, why everybody's running?
Thief! A thief!!
Catch the bastard!

Man, I'm shitting my pants
Don't
Get the bloody bastard!
Chase the scumbag!
Nooo
Where?
There!
Black balaclava on
It's him!!
Who?
The goddamn thief!
There?
He looked at me
Am I screwed?
Who?
I.
No.
Yeee
We're all gonna die!!!
Screech
Fuck
Car roaring by
We're all gonna die. We're all gonna die
No.
Tonight
What?
Die.
Yes.
Alright, fine.
So,
Die.
Die
Die
Die

Die
Die
Die
Die
t.

TWE | LVE

Interior.
Daytime.
Screen lights up in blue.
Camera slowly pans the sky-blue sky.
As it moves towards the horizon, clouds begin to obscure it all, ether and hell.
Colour changes from azure to shades of grey and finally to: Noir.
A pastiche of an Ennio Morricone soundtrack begins to play, haunting, evocative orchestral music.
A monotone voice repeats Die, Died, Die, Dead, Die, Die, Die, Die.
Cut to indoor scene, the three protagonists are seen chitchatting:
Cue, Matt...
Ella, can we borrow your car for a few hours? Me and the Boulevardier.
Sure you can, what's on?
We've been invited to Franc Ian Stine's country house art gallery.
What's he showing?
His surrealist ultra-sized paintings of wedding bouquets.
That's not art.
Matt, open your mind up to other ideas.
Like me and Bouls, do it by seeing other artists' work.
It's real, like Ells and me, you've got to keep it real, Matt.

Centre stage,
Two spotlights cross Matt, who is standing in a pose of being crucified. His head turns, he looks towards the audience.
With a stare reminiscent of the one Richard Ashcroft adopted walking down Hoxton Street, he says 'Oh Ella why has thou forsaken me. You have cut me to the quick, forsooth I love thee?'

Lights go off
Theatre goes dark

Exterior.
Night
Matt is seen sitting at a table in a derelict pub in Shoreditch.
Cue, barmaid.
And, Action!
Here we go, sunshine. Your pint of bitter, and bag of sweets.
Have you thought about smiling, cos you won't get any sympathy from me with that stare. Tell you what, buy me a drink and I'll listen to your woes. Right, that'll be: pint of bitter, £4.60; sweet, £2.76; sympathy, £7.50. I've added a tip cos I'm trying to make ends meet, so let's call it £30 sovs.
Matt looks up and shows her a photo of Ella. Have you ever seen her in here with that guy standing next to me in the photo?
Do me a favour, I see a million different people from one day to the next. But, er, yeah, I recognise her. She's an up and coming artist, her father is a leading British artist. They were in the Sunday papers when her father bought a mansion in the country and built a world-class gallery.

Elsewhere.
Deep in the Sussex countryside, Ella pulls into a lay-by:
That's it, B, we're officially lost.
We can't be far away.

Why are you always so optimistic?
I'm an artist.
It's astounding. I hope I don't start bleating, I'll let the satnav take control.
Ella, listen closely, there's music in the air!
B, there's a light!
Ella, there's a light!
Yes! There's a light over at the Franc Ian Stine's gaff.
It's just a turn to the left and then a turn to the right.
It's well secluded.
Head lights?
Ah, I see all.
I tell you, I could do with a kip.
Is there time for a kip?

THIRTE | EN

He's snoring like a broken air compressor on steroids.
Who?
You blind, Lloyd?
No, Matt. I don't think so...
The London Boulevardier!! He's napping his way to somewhere better than here.
Ah.
Eh.
Good.
By the way, I'm glad you're back.
I never left, Matt.
Yeah, that's what she said.
Ella?
How do you know?
Matt, I've been by the Boulevardier's side for longer than you can imagine.
Yeah, I imagine.
You don't.
I do.
You don't.
Fuck me, alright, no, I don't, you smart alec, you win.
Thanks.
You got it, Lloyd. What time is it?
Too late for the past and always early for the future.
10 o'clock?
PM, yes Matt.
Well, well, well.

Are you okay?
Bored as fuck, Lloyd. Boul is counting his 40-plus winks, you come and go at your pleasure, and Lady D don't usually appear till the midnight hour.
Diana?
Death, Lloyd. Death.
I know, I know she's dead, she was murdered.
No, I meant Death! Death!!
Sure.
She will come, flesh and blood. Jolly to kill us all.
That's what she said.
Who, Ella again?
No, Franc Ian Stine's wife.
Ah. By the way...
Yes, I'm glad you've finally seen it.
Lloyd?
Matt?
I don't see shit, Lloyd.
You're staring at it.
The wall?
Yes! Well, no.
Tell it like it is, Lloyd, don't get mystical, stop playing the sphincter!
The sphinx you mean?
The riddles' one. Egypt sphincter.
Sphinx.
Watch your mouth, Lloyd. Watch your mouth.
Matt, what's in front of you is an original, very rare indeed ultra-sized painting from the one and only, the master of puppets, the surrealisterest of madmen from places like Paris: Mr Franc Ian Stine in person.
Looks like a wall to me.
That's precisely the point.
I don't get it.

Art. Surrealism. Abstractions.
Can you be a bit more vague, Lloyd?
The wall. That's his painting.
Good, another freaking dauber. He friends with Hitler?
No, no, no, he's a genius! He's the ultimate inventor, the creator of everyday realities in a jar!
Innit?
He is!
So, you're telling me that's not a wall. It's a wall-size white canvas decorated with plugs and paintings. Plus, a door.
The lot.
And I didn't see it.
Precisely.
Okay, Lloyd, let me check:

And, as Matt Youth gets on his feet and approaches the canvas/wall/whatever to touch it with his own hands, the camera pans over their heads, bumps into the chandelier and zooms out of the window, and beyond, outside the building, it frames the Lloyd Hotel sign and finally shoots an ending shot of a full moon howling its malaise to the inextricable, clustered tangle of running clouds.

And that was precisely when Matt, realising the absurd creation of Mr Franc Ian Stine is actual Parisienne crap au lait stinking more than Duchamp's Fountain, sighs a long sigh and wonders with nostalgia about his heroes, Salvador Dali, Magritte, Mirò… he's so emotional that he takes a sharp turn into Romance Road and starts fantasising on 60s/70s French women beautying French movies with their attitude, their lipstick-smudged cigarettes and mascaraed tears; he almost moves thinking about the Vogue, Glamour, Cosmopolitan covers, the striped shirts, stockings, minis, the cat-eye make upped eyes. Then, Franc Ian

Stine's wall reappears into his retinas. Desperate by the current state of contemporary art, he says:
"We will always have Paris"
to the Boulevardier who suddenly spat out a rant louder than his previous rants as if he eventually found the glorious death he was seeking.
And:
End. Fin. Terminado. Go home, folks!
But is it really the end?
My dear friend?
Boul?

FOURT | EEN

It's late, Matt.
It's always later than you think, Bouls.
Where is she?
We don't know, Lloyd.
I love her, I've always loved her, Matt.
We know, Lloyd.
You both knew.
Yes.
Oh! But not having the confidence of Bouls or the smouldering suaveness of Matt, I did nothing about it. I loved her from afar. And watched as the Anglo-Italian remake of Jules et Jim, played out:
"Matt and Dave"
not playing in a theatre near you, François Truffaut had nothing to worry about. But I had the last laugh because she came to me and my Hotel to live and work and I saw her every day. I loved her, a love not returned, but love nonetheless. Only Death would keep us apart and then one morning Mr De'Ath checked in...

Cut!

What's the problem, Matt?
This scene is going on too long, it's more Ingmar Bergman than Godard.
That's if Godard exists, Matt.
Good point, Bouls.
And,

ACTION

I wish to check in. My name is Mr De'Ath. That's De'Ath.
Good morning, welcome to our hotel, Mr Deaf. Am I speaking loud enough for you?
Why are you shouting at me?
Aren't you deaf? You said you were deaf.
I can hear you perfectly well.
Okay... Mr...
I am De'Ath.
Death, the so-called Grim Reaper.
Yes, I am Death.
You said your name is De'Ath.
It is, I am Death.
So, let me get this right, your name is, De'Ath Death, the Grim Reaper.
Yes, I am Death.
And you're checking in?
No, it is you who is checking out. Take that elevator.
Where am I going?
You will find out when the doors close.
There's only one button, which way does it go? Up or down?
You will find out when the doors close.
What can I say?
Goodbye.

Screen goes completely zinc white and somewhere in the ether there is a cry of

CUT!

| 56

Angel of Darkness
Winged animal with broken
Wings
She is
Dust is
The air
Rotten
Leaves
Destroy it all
Pouring like mould from
All over the skies
Life's too short when
Death's knocking at your window pane and
Crows weep blood
Bleed
Their black eyes are
Over and out
Shut
Checking the remaining
Checks
And balances
And Yeah
Apparently you
You paid it all
Gave back your flimsy
Worn out
Soul at the counter

Used and corrupt
Filthy shadow of sorts it
Is not yours anymore
Gone
Ask the devil's clergyman he's got
No receipt
No refunds
For you for
Life is a prepaid curse you got from
Your parents didn't
Know this though:
Said the Devil of Heaven
Paradise reject
I
I who am the definitive end
I
And suddenly the skies crackled like old leafy path
Cemetery path
Petrol poured from
The depths of the oceans
Upside down
The world now
I
She repeated
Am the final glance
Black hole eating
The light's off
You!
Listen to
I
Am the last sense you ever felt
Thunderous is the air
Look at your last reflection
Stare

At the crowling hiss of you
Look:
Beware.

FIF | TEEN

She's here, she's here!!
 Now, stop howling and drooling like a dog, Matt.
 But...
 Stop!
 She's arrived!!
 Okay, all this excitement is making me sick.
 Aren't you happy, Boul?
 What?
 Happy.
 Happiness makes me sad, Matt.
 Say it again?
 Happiness makes me...
 Yeeeeeeeee
 I swear to god, I
 Which one?
 Oh, well,
 The Jewish one?
 Could be.
 Christian?
 ...
 Muslim?
 Aren't they all the same?
 So... an Indu bunch?
 Enough, Matt.
Yeah you're right, Boul, let's not waste time. We came here for a reason. We waited the night for it. We did all we did for it and now she's finally here.
 I doubt it. Besides,

She's he-re! H-e-r-e!
Who? Who on earth, Matt?? Whooooooo??
De'Ath! Didn't you hear?
No.
She's checking in.
Impossible.
Why?
It's too early.
It's past eleven now.
Precisely.
Precisely what?
The worst only happens after 2 am.
Is that a rule?
Matt, please.
Please what?
Please.
Okay, it's a rule, but it's a faulty one cuz she's here.
Wrong. Though, my calculations show that she can also arrive at specific hours like:
- between 3 pm and midnight in winter
- between 9:30 and midnight in summer
- Closed on Sundays

You mean when it gets dark.
Ish. And, closed on Sundays.
Innit?
Yes.
Makes sense. And yet... why don't you ask her?
Why don't you shut up, Matt?
Look, she's waving at you.
She is?
She is.
She is?
She's there.

Ah.
Aha!
Right. Should I feel a shiver or something?
Nah, Boul, that's fictional rubbish you hear in fictional stories...
Silly me, I thought we were inside a movie.
A book, you mean.
No, no, no, stop disputing everything I say, I meant a book, Matt.
See?
Holy crap, holy bloody Jesus Christ crap, you're confusing me!
It's a book.
A movie!
A boooook!!
A moooooveyyyyyyy!!!
A cinematic adaptation of a novel played in all theaters from March?
Okay, alright, it's a facking tell-me then!!
Don't get all heated up, Boul.
I'M NOT!!!
Boul, let me tell you this:
I don't want to hear it.
you are a tiny tad quite upset.
Fuck off.
See? Your language is derailing down the Matt Youth path. You're one fuck away from becoming a villain.
Like you?
Precisely me. Boul, you need to relax, embrace time, and welcome De'Ath.
...
...
...
Matt, before I start crying, where the hell are we?
Sir, you're at the Lloyd Hotel, the almost best hotel in town. The excellentest of differently-named Excelsiors. The jewel in the

crown. The getting-there awarded "It Don't Shit Hotel of the Year", the,
   I need a bathroom window...
   Yeah, Lloyd, we're losing the audience.
   Matt, I...
   You?
   Lloyd,
   Sir?
   please put an end to this indisentangleable argument.
   Okay, Matt is right.
   Do what?
   Matt is right, sir.
   No way.
   Yes way.
   Aha, see? See?
   Shut up, Matt. Lloyd?
   Sir?
   Can you confirm you just checked in a certain... person?
   Who do you mean, sir?
   A lady without a face, fully hooded-up, hollow like a starless night and floating around like a hovercrafting hoover without a pilot?
   Lady De'Ath, you mean.
   Das the one, Lloyd. Bravo.
   Thanks, Matt.
   Thanks, Matt. (with a funny voice). Ridiculous.
   It's the truth.
   Whatever.
   Time has come, Boul, embrace it.
   Like you do, Matt?
   Yup!
   Okay.
   Cool.

Cooler to me.
Coolerer to me too plus one.
Great.
Marvelously, colossally grand.
...
...
...
So?
So what, Mr London Boulevardier?
Aren't you going to introduce her to us?

SIXTE | EN

Gramophone scratching music off of a dusty vinyl.
Real. Folk. Blues.
Cowboys.
It's a western, babe!
Said no one as Matt stood up and said:

1966, 3 am.
I was walking the murky streets of London, Camden Docks, Locks?, whatever, it smelled like danger, dodgy as fuck, so insanely vicious I was literally shitting my pants. *(ugh...)*
All in all, the night was quiet. People snored their issues down within the broken walls of their broken homes and I was lost around a Damask carpet of soulless streets. Only the sharpest knives lived the town at that hour. Wanksta was graffiting bricks like there was no tomorrow. None Here was nowhere in sight doing something nobody knew. I bet my girl was warming some stranger's bed mattress while my friend Vincenzo dug a motherfucking hole, one so goddamn deep to end up inside the vault of this or that Lloyds bank.
The London Boulevardier was after the money.
What money?
The money.
Geez, I was so knackered I would have gladly died on the spot, and I was just about to take a leap into the canal when a boy emerged from the thick mantle of drizzle. I said, *Nothing* and he precisely replied *Nothing* back to me. So, I kept walking my way

away from that shithole and that's exactly when the scoundrel yelled:
Man!
Boy!
Listen to this:
And he blew his soul inside a rusty harmonica, *help me baby, help me darling*, he sang, guitar in hand like a shotgun, only it was blues, babe.
Help Me, Sonny Boy Williamson! I shouted with a grimace that showed some sort of excitement.
No can do, boss. My name is Sonny Boy Patterson.
Ah.
I replied, and lit a cigarette that didn't smoke, so much was the fog wrapping us tight like falafel wraps.
And
Bang, Bang!
Bang.
...
Was I dead, de'Ath?
Sorry, who are you?
Me? I'm Matt Youth, babe.
You go call babe your sister, mister.
Oh yeah?
Oh. Yeah.
OH YEAH?
Oh Yeah. Period.
Ah. Okay... I'm sorry, de'Ath.
You bet.
I don't.
Right, enough with this bollocks detour.
It was all true, I swearish!
Shut up, Youth.
I'm zipped.
I need to have a word with:

SEVENTEE | N

Bang! Bang! Bang!

Always with the explosions, Matt. Now, the Boulevardier, he is sensitive while you are simply bombastic which is why he and I are going travelling together tomorrow morning so it's Ciao baby.

Bang! Bang! Bang!
There's someone at the door.

Ella strolls over and with a hello, and bonjour, she opens the door.
It was black, no light entered, it must be nighttime she thought, it was like staring into the abyss. No, more like looking into a gaping pitch black maw.
She half expected to see miners emerging and dispersing, she could hear echoes coming from the depths of this black hole. The echoes became more solid. It was as if someone was walking towards her, she listened as the footsteps grew louder and suddenly stopped and a figure dressed all in black stepped out and looking down at her said
I wish to check - in. My name is De'Ath.
Fuck me, thought Ella, this geezer must be at least 7 foot tall. Looking up she replied,
Follow me to the reception.

I wish to check - in. My name is De'Ath.
Er, sorry sir I may have misheard. Did you, did you say Death?
Yes I did. I am De'Ath.

So let me get this right, your name is Death.
Yes, I am he.
And you are checking out.
No.
So, you're checking in?
Yes. I am. It is you who are checking out.
When you say I'm checking out what does that mean?
I will explain in simple terms what you are to do. The existential, you may ponder at your leisure. Now:
Take elevator No.3a and...
Mr De'Ath, er... there's no 3a.
'My time is my time', De'Ath stands at his full height, towering over the reception desk, 'I do not provide insight, nor explanations. And I do not negotiate. You will enter elevator No.3a, press the button with the arrow down symbol on it. Enjoy the journey.'

The receptionist, placing his pass key on the desk, walks across the lobby and without looking back enters the elevator. A Foreign National, passing on his way to find the pool, swears the receptionist began throwing guitar shapes like he was on stage at Hammersmith Palace. He also says he thought he heard someone say 'Going down'

#7 | TYEIGHT

Meet me whenever you want
  X o'clock
  At the Mo
  Dern
  Tate Turbine
  Hall
  I'll be the one
  With a Rose in hand
  Charlotte
  Not you
  It's my Lidl rose
  Pink
  Or so they sold it
  To me
  Anyways,
  Call me if you don't
  Come!
  I'll be the one
  With a jacket colour
  Cognac
  French like
  Paillettes
  Wow, Matt, you really know how
  To lose the audience and
  Silver
  That's my glittery jacket's colour anyway,
  You can't miss me

Ella
Unless I can't
Come
So meet me there tomorrow
Or don't
We can discuss art
Yours and mine
Cause what other art is there to see?
I wonder
How long will it take
For you
Or me
Or you
To crack the walls of the Mo
Dern
Tate
Uh?
We can talk about that
Cause what else do you want to discuss?
Me?
I'm not that impor
Tant
Unless you make me
Feel like a star
You are
I know
But let's see it tomorrow
Y o'clock
Somewhere around the
Turbine Hall
Does this invitation sound weird to you?
Am I mad?
No
I'm just Matt

Matt Youth, babe
The lamest cowboy on Earth
A disinfluencer of sorts
Number one of all number twos
So I say sorry to you
For calling you babe,
Babe
That's only my way of trying to sound
Somehow
Somewhat
Remotely
Cool
Interesting
With a touch of mystery
Or dangerous
Edgy?
Fuck me, I'm not
I'm a professional disappointer of ex
Pec
Tations so
Please don't bring any
Just come as you are
No make up
Take your time
Hurry up
The choice is yours
Don't be late
And I'll be the one
(fat chance)
I promise (nah...)
It's gonna be fun
Innit?
So, say it:

Yay or Nay
Uh?

A | RTZONE

Rose, oh, Rose...
Who's Rose? You mean Ella.
Charlotte.
Danielle?
Michelle!
Yes, yes, Michelle! Michelle, ma belle.
No need to start dancing, Boul.
But the London Boulevardier suddenly felt uplifted from any fear, pain or other material concern and started swinging the room like a swan in love. A drunken swan in love.
Michelle, ma belle
Sont les mots qui vont tres bien ensemble
Tres bien ensemble
He sang happy as ever and so did Matt, finally letting go a long thread of feelings he kept tangled in his pockets for a lifetime or two:
I love you, I love you, I love you
That's all I want to say
Until I find a way
He sang as the Boulevardier kept dancing like a pro, tip tapping around, twisting the tiles, pirouetting the right left and centre of the room.
I will say the only words I know that you'll understand
My Michelle...
They concluded singing back to back, both thinking about their belle, Rose, Ella, Michelle, Claire, it didn't matter anymore. Love plays weird tricks on people sometimes.

And that's when Lloyd applauded an enthusiastic applause that shook the dust off the silence and brightened up the room. Don't get lost down memory lane, my friends.

He said, a split second before someone or something banged a deaf KNOCK that echoed inside everyone's soul like a shiver.

Ella...

EIGHTE | EN

Ella?
Matt?
Boul?
Lloyd?
Fackin heaven, the whole bunch of losers, in my fav hotel, at once.
And you are?
De'Ath.
As in...
De'Ath.
Innit?
Matt, please stop bothering our guest and sit the fuck down.
You got it, Boul.
Sir, I...
Lloyd, haven't you done enough damage already?
Such as...?
Say no more.
Sure. Thank you, sir.
Boulevardier?
Ella?
Nothing. I just wanted to ask you about... but let's not get there.
Where?
Oh, Mrs De'Ath, it's really not important.
No Mrs for me, please. It's De'Ath that's it.
So... Mr? Miss?
Both.

Oh, you're a they.
No, I'm a me!
You undecided?
I'm not. I'm De'Ath. De'Ath!
Pick a letter!
What bloody letter?
Ah, this is going to be fun, trust me!
I don't.
Oh my, it's such a spree, such a spree! Pick one letter:
Holy Hell... no!
LGBTQABCDEFGH...
I said I'm De'Ath! De'Ath, De'Ath, De'Ath!!!
Tut-tut, don't be that guy.
Ella?
Matt?
Would you please avoid making him angry, for Christ's sake?!
Him? It hasn't decided yet.
HE DID!!! Forget about this gender bullshit!!!
It's not bullsh
HEM. HEM. AHEM.
Yes, De'Ath?
You must be the London Boulevardier.
In person.
The one who climbs out of bathroom windows.
I thoroughly deny all the accusations, Your Honour.
So, what's the story?
Mourning Glory ahaha.
And you are Matt Youth. The cretin who believes he's funny.
I...
Shut up.
...

Now, if it was up to me, this conversation would have been over since before you were born. Too bad that there is only one elevator 3a in this hotel. And it's pretty crowded at the moment.

We could take the stairs.
Matt? Wtf?
Ella?
Please, Miss, let me handle this.
It's Mrs, Mr De'Ath.
Mrs? Mrs?? Since when???
London Boulevardier, sit down! Please let's not lose focus.
Sorry, De'Ath. (Since wheeeeen??)
Enough! Where were we?
Stairs.
Right. If Matt fancies trying alternative routes to elevator 3a, he can certainly take the Stairway to Never, it's just around the corner.
Holy Moly, this is a good one, De'Ath!
Matt, do I look like joking?
Boul, is he not...
He's not. Definitely not.
Mr De'Ath, sir, I'm afraid I have a bookful of tasks to be performed before tomorrow morning. I shall leave you to your pleasant conversation, if I may.
Lloyd, you ain't going nowhere. You set this whole thing up so sit your ass down and watch.
He set it up?
Yes, Matt.
How do you know?
I'm De'Ath, I know shit.
He set what? Lloyd? What the hell did you do?
I... sir... what time is it?
It's too late o'clock.
Thanks, De'Ath.
Oh, don't thank me, people. The worst has yet to come.

NI | NETEEN

Coming up, said the disembodied voice, sounding like a melange of Alexa and Marlene Dietrich.
Excusi says a passenger elbowing his way down the carriage, let me through, I'm an artist.
A con artist, says the Boulevardier throwing his arms out as Vincenzo hugs him.
Good to see you
You too
And you
Hugh
Me
No Hugh
You who
You know it feels like Dèjá Vu

TICKETS! Says a rather tall train inspector making his way down

There's something absurdly wrong with this, firstly I was in hospital and then in an elevator, and you know how much I hate them. I had a waking dream about being a birdwatcher and we were waiting for the elusive Birdboy but he didn't turn up.
Now I'm on a train and the ticket inspector is De'Ath.
Where is Ella, my mate Matt, Lloyd?

You will see them when they too transition to a different plane. Until then I am De'Ath and I have come for...
Me! Says Vincenzo, it's not his time, there was a mixup and the notice went to the wrong Death.

I am De'Ath.
Of course you are and it's time for us to go...

There is a loud beep beeping. The Boulevardier thinks he hears someone say
  We're losing him...
  ...et...t...paddles...
And again the curtain comes down and all is black again.

| *^

Enjoy.
Your.
Sickness.

Pronounced by a side wall, maybe the ceiling?, no, it was the fireplace, yes, to slur those three words and dots with a gravelly sombre tone that tasted of: afterlife.
Chills scratched everyone's but De'Ath's back. Someone cried like a girl (Matt), others snored their panic away (the Boulevardier). Lloyd still swears he never ever heard any sort of noises/voices/rants/intimidations coming from this or that dubious wall or the occasional shady corner of his Hotel, the Lloyd Hotel. *My place is not haunted, my place is not haunted!* he shrilled hysterically as Ella, who apparently everybody knew to be dead from something like I don't know, ages, didn't make a move, so intensely absorbed she was in sipping the blandest brew ever tea-ed. Or maybe it was the other way around. Or maybe nothing you read in the previous 12 lines ever happened. Or...
Did it?

NIN | ETEEN

Elevator up
  Elevator down
  Elevator up
  Elevator down
  Elevator up
  Ele
Facking heaven, stop it!
vator down
Matt, you push that bloody button again and I swear to Satan...
Uh?
Don't.
This?
Nooo!!!!
Down
Come here you motherf
Up
Ahhhhh
Down
Stop messing with elevator 3a!! It's my favourite, you're gonna break it.
  And you are?
  De'Ath.
  Deaf? You're deaf?
  I'm De'Ath, De'Ath!!
  I HEARD YOU. Geez...
  What the fuck, Youth. What made you think that getting on elevator No.3a was a good idea?

Well... I was getting bored, the Elly was free so...
Helly?
Elly-vator, innit?
What's wrong with you?
Don't know what you're talking about.
Get back into the living room, now!
Nah...
Nah?
I like it here. Love the custom lift buttons you had installed by the way.
They're standard.
Standard my ass, look: 1 - Jolly Roger; 2 - Skull the Bully Bull; 3 - Jon Bone Jovi; 4 -
Point taken, they get creative at the HQ sometimes.
Can I have one?
One of what?
One of those.
Forget it. The lift buttons are copyrighted.
What about this?
No.
This?
Never.
First one on the right?
No. No. And no, not even number 8.
Okay.
Good.
That?
ENOUGH!!
Bummer. You're boringer than death.
I AM De'Ath!!
What happens if I press *"down plus ultra"*?
You...

Too late. As the elevator plunged into the bliss of nowhere fast without a return ticket at SpaceX rocket speed, just because Matt (who else?) pressed the only button no one ever dared to touch for a reason (there was a Post-it® saying "never ever touch this button for a reason"), everybody was la-di-da and fuck me I lost my bullet train of thought goddammit I don't even remember why I was typing this nonsense story into this nonsense book nobody not even my mum will ever buy for Christ's sake, ahhhhhh!
I mean
Aaaaaahhhhhhhhhhhhhhhhh

Calm down.
Down?
Yes. Wait, no.
Up?
Matt, this joke isn't funny anymore.
Where are we?
We aren't.
Cool. Am I De'ath?
In your dreams. I am De'Ath!
No need to brag about it, dude.
Whatever.
Nevermind.
Anyhow, you said dead, not deaf, right Matt? You're dead.
Wait, you saying I'm a dad?
A dad? No. Why should you...
No fucking shit, De'Ath! I can't be a dad. No. No. No. No. No. No. No. No. No. No. No. No. No. No.
Matt?
No. No. No. No. No. No. No. No. No. No. No. No. No. No. No. No. No. No. No. No.
Matt, pull yourself together!

Please, take me with you.
Where?
Hell, bring me down to hell.
Don't make me laugh. I can't have children, I'd rather be suicidally successful, I'd rather be murdered she wrote, killed, shot dead, dead, dead, dead!!! Take me away.
No can do. I work solo.
I will be silent. Invisible. Matt Youth no more. Quiet as a lamb. Are you done with this charade?
Put me on a cross, like Geeza.
When was the last time you had sex?
By... myself?
Facking heaven you're thick as a brick. With a woman!
Well... I...
So, no, You don't have kids, how can you have kids if you don't hanky-panky with a woman?
Good point. *Oof...* thank goodness. I thought dying was pretty harsh but when you told me I was the father of some creep... *eww...*
Marvellous. Now, shut the fuck up. Don't you see I'm busy trying to fix the elevator?
It's broken? We stuck in hell?
Matt?
De'Ath?
What part of shut the fuck up you didn't understand?
The...
Tut-tut. Ah, finally, jackpot!
Fixed?
Good as before you.
Bravo!
You got it.
What's that?

No no no no no no, you don't dare to touch another button again. You screwed my lift already. I promise you, You will never happen again.
It. You mean, it!
No, I mean, you.
And

Ting!
Said the elevator, stopping exactly back at:
Lloyd's Hotel, 11:59 pm, lounge.
A jet-black military boot kicked Matt Youth's ass off of elevator No.3a and he tumbled over the London Boulevardier, waking him from the deepest of sleep*Zzzz*
Zzzz

TWEN | TEEN

HOTEL LLOYD
   The ending innit

PREVIOUSLY
   Lacuna

PREVIOUSLY
   The plot having lost its way is retired with prejudice

NOW
   Lloyd (just Lloyd) appalled at the narrative of the last chapter decided to complete his biographical film of the London painter and socialite "The London Boulevardier". He had written the screenplay, adapted from his original script about the rapprochement between Matt Youth and the Boulevardier after their estrangement when faced with the reality that they were both in love with Ella.

LATER
   Lloyd, sitting in a canvas chair with DICTATOR stencilled on the back, a souvenir from the time the Boulevardier encouraged the audience at the Soho theatre (where Vlad Smythz was performing) to storm the theatre stage and defenestrate the fucker while the Old Bill were making human shields of themselves to protect the former dictator Vlad Smythz, is pensive.
   I miss those adventures, he thinks out loud as he walks out of the room carrying his chair. Raising his hand, the set goes quiet,

the actors still on stage stop talking. Coughing slightly, Lloyd exclaims, Cut. It's a wrap!

There is spontaneous applause. As the crew and talent walk past him some to their trailers, some to other movies on the lot, he returns high fives, shakes hands, kisses and nothing for as he turns to walk to his trailer, what appears to be a weaponised microphone is pointed at him by a clearly deranged reporter who says, 'The readers of Zite and Zounds magazine are eager for any morsel of truth and/or gossip and/or lies about the relationship(s) between the Boulevardier, Matt Youth and the so-called love interest, Ella.

Lloyd is ice cool, channelling Paul Newman in cool hand Luke says, fella, is that a microphone in your hand or are you just pleased to see me? To which the reporter replies, are you having a laugh?, thrusting his phallic device into the air.

I see, concludes Lloyd, you are pleased to see me.

A crowd of people had gathered around Lloyd. Turning to them he announces: Ladies and Gentleman, standing before me and you, with a metaphorical dick in his hand, is GW Sh'Ark the so-called Art critic for the Daily Mail, a pundit who knows fuck all about art but it doesn't stop him having an opinion.

It's a free country, says Sh'Ark.

Is it, asks Lloyd. They call you the Great White Shark...

Don't call me that, says Sh'Ark.

... because there's always blood in the water when you are around?

...

If you want an understanding of the relationship between the three of them, you are welcome to attend the premiere.

Opening Curzon Cinema Soho Thursday

TWE | NTY ONE

And, CUUUUT!
Unbelievable, what is this crap? Lloyd? Lloyd?? Where is that good for nothing when you need him? I have De'Ath on the payroll, we rented a bloody colossal Hotel for this shit play and you tell me what?
Ella has to be in the film.
Oh, don't encourage him, Mister Boulevardier.
I agree.
No, Matt, you definitely don't agree, Matt. You barely know what we're talking about, Matt.
Money?
No, not money! Money's too much to mention, we have a list of sponsors so long we could make a film out of that credits' scroll.
Ella. We were talking about Ella.
I agree.
You two bloody fools, I was just about to wrap this insult-to-cinema and send it to Hollywood, you can't be serious!
Look, mate, this is very important for me, and for Matt, isn't it, Matt?
Er...
Matt?
Boul?
Right. Right. I, the London Boulevardier, refuse to continue shooting this film if we're not talking about Ella.
Who the hell is Ella???
Lloyd, do you mind explaining the whereabouts of this perfectly intricate situation to the director?
There you were, you bast...

It would be my pleasure, sir.
I DON'T WANT TO HEAR IT!
Okay. Matt?
Boul?
You tell him.
Mmm...
Tell him!
I... She... Er...
I thought you were a friend, Matt.
And I thought this was a bleak story about death and growing old and suicide and challenging the Grim Reaper every New Year's Eve of every Year till death would tear us apart..
Innit, now?
Innit, Boul? You talking Cockney street slang now?
I am.
Great. And yeah, that's precisely the crap we sold to the producers.
Mr director, please...
No, you two please. You were looking for a job, and then you begged for it, and cried, and moaned, and heaven knows I gave you the job!
In fact, that's how it started.
What. What started, Mr Boulevardier?
The Ella story.
Aha! Now I remember!
Jesus, Matt, you were there...
Mister Director, let me explain:
Lloyd, please don't.
They were looking for a job,
And that we fucking got already.
And then they found a job.
Thanks to me!

And then they found themselves a girlfriend, and they hated their guts and, heaven knows, they were miserable then and
Wooo
Matt?
Don't facking tell me.
But you know the story already.
Spoiler!!!
But you know the story already.
Yeah, don't wanna recall.
Lloyd, finish what you started.
It would be my pleasure, sir.
Lallallallallallallalla
What is he muttering?
He just doesn't want to hear, sir.
Hear what?
Thanks for asking, mister Director. So: Matt told the Boulevardier, and the Boulevardier told Matt about Ella.
Innit?
And the conversation went like:
'Shut up.'
'Okay.'
'I want out.'
'No, I want out first.'
'Great, so Ella's mine.'
'No, I want out of this job, can't work with a treacherous cheater like you.'
'Marvellous. Suit yourself. Be poor.'
'You know what, Boul? I'll get you fired.'
'You wish.'
'I do.'
'You don't.'
'I do said I do, don't I?'
'Well, you can't fire me cause I quit.'
'Pretty rocknroll, uh, mate?'

'Mate?'
'Mate.'
And that resulted in a physical fistfight which nobody won nor barely got close to winning. Why, you ask? Cause Ella knocked at the open door, found the two arguing and ketchup spilled on the floor. So, she ran down the stairs in tears and, Ubering herself out of there... but the rest is history. Besides:
They lost their jobs, got broke again, and forever they were, looking for a job, begging for a job, begging for a girl, working like dogs and heaven knows they were miserabler now.

Clap - clap - clap

Bravo, said the director. Only, we're not shooting that kind of film. Not on my watch.
So, turn the other way, mate. Look!
Where?
Now!! He's distracted, go ahead, guys, bag him!
Oh, Lloyd, don't you see?
What?
This thing is creating trouble only. Boul, are you seriously suggesting we shall pretend Last Night at the Lloyd Hotel is actually a love story?
You got it, Youth.
I'm outta here.
You sold out. If Ella could listen to you, she would undoubtedly pick me and be ashamed she even considered the remote, never-going-to-happen possibility of giving you a chance.
Now, hold your horses, cowboy.
I have my mock Glock ready to fire, Youth.
Aw, don't get me started.
Start. Please.
Okay, Mr London Boulevardier. Or, should I call you

Suspense

Dave?

A handful of jaws dropped all around the room. The director was incredulous. Lloyd turned the other way. De'Ath's head popped off its hood for a second, to see things clearly.

Holy fucking Moly. Sounds like someone's looking for a good old artsy duel, said the Boulevardier.

THE DUEL

LLOYD

Cashier with a pistol. Green acountant visor on. Loyal friend, servant, butler, bartender of the London Boulevardier. Apparently mild temper, he fiercely fight like a mad dog when accused of running a properly-haunted Hotel.
The Lloyd Hotel.

WEAPON OF CHOICE:
VINTAGE COLT .45

the London
BOULEVARDIER

DRESSED IN A GREEN SUIT AND HOLDING A
FULLY LOADED CAP GUN STUFFED WITH CAP-
GUN AMMOS, HE'S A MAN YOU DON'T WANNA
MESS WITH. KING OF THE ART SCENE, HE'S
BEEN AVOIDING HIS NEW SHOW FOR DECADES.
THOUGH, HE AIN'T EVER AVOIDING
A GOOD-OLD DUEL

WEAPON OF CHOICE:
MOCK CLOCK

Matt Youth

MULTI MEDIA WANNABE ARTIST.
HOPELESS ROMANTIC. HE ACTS LIKE A
GANGSTA WHEN IN FACT HE'S THE N. 1 OF
NUMBER 2s. BEST AT WHAT HE DOES
WORST. FULL TIME PRO LOSER.
MALE. BEWARE FOR YOUTH.
MATT YOUTH

WEAPON OF CHOICE:
IS THAT... A BANANA?

DE'ATH

BEAUTIFULLY LETHAL LIKE A RED
LIPSTICKED LIPS KISS ON HEELS
SO HIGH THAT YOU'D FEAR A
SECOND RIDE ON THOSE LONG
LEGS. WHAT WERE WE TALKING
ABOUT? AH, DEATH. NO
DE'ATH!

WEAPON OF CHOICE:
PERFECTLY SHARPENED SHYTHE

Ella

Beautiful. As. Ever.
A thread of long blond hair drops over
her right eye curtaining her sadness.
She appears to be screaming: don't. Please.
No more ketchup has to be bled in our lives.
She says that and:

WEAPON OF CHOICE:
SINGLE BAT OF EYELASHES

| 666

Her face
Pure
Grace
On neck
Like a painting
You can't stop digging
Your soul into her
Brushstrokes are wild
When she smiles
It's heavenly hell
Burst like flames
The love of
Lovers
For her
Never-ending spell
Where was I?
Ah
Her face
Suddenly caves in
Like Atlantis at 3 pm,
Sinks
Into blissful pitch
Black
Hole
Crunching light and matter
At once
Her eyes are
Gone

The head now wrapped into a hood
Black hood
Hi,
I'm De'Ath she says
You what?
You'll rot
In hell
And back
You don't say
Ella? Ella?
She's no more
Give her back, Death!
But I am
De'Ath
Angel of Hell
Been there the whole time
Waited for you year after year
The two of you
Same place, same time
Midnight
December 30th
My last Uber ride
Ella…
Guys
We didn't want to…
Didn't see you…
Shhhh
Uh?
Check your watch
What time is it?
It's too late o'clock
Again?
For good.

You don't say
I do
You don't
I do
You don't
I... Enough!
...
Now,
Get ready for:

BANG!

BANG BANG!

SHHHHH INNNG!

KATANA SOUND
COURTESY OF JAMES LAWRENCE,
PAPERBACK SOUND EFFECTS ENGINEER

BANG!!
BANG!
BANG! BANG!

ARTZO | NE

The white light was dazzling her, she could hear voices, some of them close, some so far away. It was as if the light was calling her. Someone, a man, said '11:58 am. She's gone.'
What did it mean? Who is he? Where was she?
She could hear Matt, in his lyrical Italian voice, say, 'What do you mean by that? She can't be?'
She could hear Dave, losing his cool, 'Answer the fucking question..?'
Matt, trying to calm him down; he was only just able to contain the urge to weep uncontrollably.
'Dave, mate, it's his job it's not personal.'
The man in a white coat says, 'She's gone.'
She thought, 'Who's gone.'
Dave asks, 'Gone where. Where's she gone?'
'She died. Mr Boulevardier, I'm sorry for your loss.'
She watches as the white coat walks through the door, she can see a bald patch on the top of his head.
Why am I looking down on him, the white light becomes brighter and she suddenly realises, 'I'm dead. I can float.' The white light is calling her gently, she knows what she should do.
Matt and Dave are holding each other and crying, she floats through them, she is all love, she enters the white light and as she does so, it blinks out.
Matt smiles
Dave smiles
She loved them both
And...

DAS | IT

Silence.
Roaring. Bleeding. Silence.
The duel's over, said no one. Dead.

Around the rooms of the Lloyd Hotel a persistent nothingness pierced eardrums like there was no tomorrow. The haunted walls kept schtum for the very first time since page one;
Ghosts, phantoms, spectres, apparitions, wraiths, shadows, presences, bodachs, Doppelgängers, duppies, spooks, phantasms, shades, revenants, visitants, wights, eidolons, manes and... where was I? Ah,
All those entities observed the scene in

Silence.
Roaring. Bleeding. Silence.

For a moment, it felt like the world held its breath and watched what was happening on its crust. Zooming in all its way from Nowhere to the Lloyd Hotel, it entered the lobby and;
The sulphuric gunpowder fog gradually vanished, revealing nothing but bad news. Destruction. Human hopelessness. If you were a passerby passing by the Hotel at that time, you would have probably thought best to get the *beep* away from that hopeless crime scene. Fast. And you would.
But when you were just about to shut the door behind and leave this story forever, something like a hand moved, and one face encrusted with blood emerged from the mist:

"I'm still stand-ish"

It hissed.

to be continued...

or not.

Printed in Great Britain
by Amazon